The Tale of Tommy Fox

Arthur Scott Bailey

Copyright © 2023 Culturea Editions
Text and cover : © public domain
Edition : Culturea (Hérault, 34)
Contact : infos@culturea.fr
Print in Germany by Books on Demand
Design and layout : Derek Murphy
Layout : Reedsy (https://reedsy.com/)
ISBN : 9791041953059
Légal deposit : September 2023

The Tale Of Tommy Fox

I

TOMMY ENJOYS HIMSELF

Tommy Fox was having a delightful time. If you could have come upon him in the woods you would have been astonished at his antics. He leaped high off the ground, and struck out with his paws. He opened his mouth and thrust his nose out and then clapped his jaws shut again, with a snap. Tommy burrowed his sharp face into the dead leaves at his feet and tossed his head into the air. And then he jumped up and barked just like a puppy.

If you could have hid behind a tree and watched Tommy Fox you would have said that he was playing with something. But you never could have told what it was, because you couldn't have seen it. And you may have three guesses now, before I tell you what it was that Tommy Fox was playing with. ... It was a feather! Yes—Tommy had found a downy, brownish feather in the woods, which old Mother Grouse had dropped in one of her flights. And Tommy was having great sport with it, tossing it up in the air, and slapping and snapping at it, as it drifted slowly down to the ground again.

He grew quite excited, did Tommy Fox. For he just couldn't help making believe that it was old Mother Grouse herself—and not merely one of her smallest feathers that he had found. And he leaped and bounded and jumped and tumbled about and made a great fuss over nothing but that little, soft, brownish feather.

There was something about that feather that made Tommy's nose twitch and wrinkle and tremble. Tommy sniffed and sniffed at the bit of down, for he liked the smell of it. It made him feel very hungry. And at last he felt so hungry that he decided he would go home and see if his mother had brought him something to eat. So he started homewards.

I must explain that Tommy lived with his mother and that their house was right in the middle of one of Farmer Green's fields, not far from the foot of

Blue Mountain. When Tommy was quite small his mother had chosen that place for her house, which was really a den that she had dug in the ground. By having her house in the center of the field she knew that no one could creep up and catch Tommy when he was playing outside in the sunshine. Now Tommy was older, and had begun to roam about in the woods and meadows alone. But Mrs. Fox liked her home in the field, and so she continued to live there.

Tommy was so hungry, now, and in such a hurry to reach home, that you might think that he would have gone straight toward his mother's house. But he didn't. He trotted along a little way, and suddenly gave a sidewise leap which carried him several feet away from the straight path he had been following. Again he trotted ahead for a short distance. And then he wheeled around and ran in a circle. And after he had made the circle he jumped to one side once more, and ran along on an old tree which had fallen upon the ground. He was not playing. No!—Tommy Fox was just trying to obey his mother. Ever since he had been big enough to wander off by himself she had told him that he must never go anywhere without making jumps and circles. "It takes longer," she said; "but it is better to do that way, because it makes it hard for a dog to follow you. If you ran straight ahead, Farmer Green's dog could go smelling along in your footsteps, and if he didn't actually catch you he could follow you right home and then we would have to move, to say the least."

Tommy was so afraid of dogs that he almost never forgot to do just as his mother told him. He was half-way home and passing through a clump of evergreens, when he suddenly stopped. The wind was blowing in his face, and brought to his nostrils a smell that made him tremble. It was not a frightened sort of tremble, but a delicious, joyful shiver that Tommy felt. For he smelled something that reminded him at once of that feather with which he had been playing. And Tommy stood as still as a statue and his sharp eyes looked all around. At first he could see nothing. But in a minute or two he noticed something on the ground, beneath one of the evergreen trees. He had looked at it carefully several times; and each time he had decided that it was only an old tree-root. But now he saw that he had been mistaken.

Yes! It was old Mother Grouse herself!

II

JOHNNIE GREEN GOES HUNTING

When Tommy Fox discovered old Mother Grouse crouched beneath the evergreen tree he grew hungrier than ever. And he decided that he would catch Mrs. Grouse and eat her on the spot.

Tommy had never caught a grouse. But his mother had brought home some of old Mother Grouse's relations for him to eat; and Tommy knew of nothing that tasted any better.

He thought that old Mother Grouse must be sleeping, she was so still. And he did not mean to wake her if he could help it—at least, not until he had caught her. So Tommy flattened himself out on his stomach and began to creep towards her, very slowly and very carefully. He didn't make the slightest noise. And soon he had stolen so close to old Mother Grouse that he was just about to spring up and rush upon her. Then all at once there was the most terrible noise. It was almost as loud as thunder, and it seemed to Tommy that the ground was rising right up in front of him. He was so startled that he fell over backward. And his heart thumped and pounded against his ribs.

The next moment Tommy Fox felt very sheepish, for he realized that the noise was nothing but the beating of old Mother Grouse's wings against the air. And instead of the ground rising, it was old Mother Grouse herself who had jumped up and sailed away. She hadn't been asleep. She had seen him all the time.

And she had just waited until she saw that Tommy was trying to catch her before she flew off.

Old Mother Grouse didn't fly far. She perched in a tree just a little way off and sat there and looked down at Tommy Fox and chuckled to herself. She knew that she was perfectly safe. And though Tommy Fox trotted up to the tree where she sat and stared longingly up at her she wasn't the least bit worried. For she knew quite well that Tommy couldn't climb a tree.

Tommy felt very peevish. He was so hungry! And he couldn't help thinking how good old Mother Grouse would have tasted. He couldn't reach her now. But still he didn't go along toward home. He simply couldn't keep his greedy eyes off fat old Mother Grouse! And he squatted down beside a bush and stared at her.

Old Mother Grouse didn't mind that. She just stared back at Tommy Fox; and she didn't say a word to him, which somehow made Tommy still more peevish.

How long Tommy would have stayed there it would be hard to tell. But in a little while something happened that sent him home on the run. If Mrs. Grouse and Tommy had been looking out as sharply as they generally did, Farmer Green's boy never could have crept up so close to them. But they were so busy staring at each other that they never saw Farmer Green's boy at all.

Now, Johnnie Green had his gun with him, for he was hunting grouse. He did not see Tommy Fox at all, because Tommy was hidden behind the bush. But Johnnie Green saw old Mother Grouse; and almost as soon as he saw her he fired.

The old shot-gun made a tremendous roar. The woods rang and echoed with the noise. And Tommy Fox saw a cloud of feathers float down from the limb where old Mother Grouse had been sitting. But old Mother Grouse herself flew away. The shot had knocked out some of her tail-feathers, but hadn't hurt her at all.

It all happened very quickly. And Tommy Fox felt himself leaping high in the air. He was so frightened that he had jumped almost out of his skin. And he ran and ran, and ran faster than he had ever run before in all his rather short life.

Johnnie Green saw him run. But his gun wasn't loaded now, and he couldn't shoot. And he didn't have his dog with him, either. It was lucky for Tommy Fox that there was no dog there. For Tommy was so scared that he forgot all about jumping sideways, and running in circles, as his mother had taught him. He just ran straight for his home in the middle of the big field; and when he got there he scurried through the door and scampered inside; and he never came out again all that day.

III

TOMMY FOX LEARNS TO HUNT

Tommy Fox was hunting crickets in the field near his mother's house. Being a young fox, not much more than half-grown, Tommy knew very little of hunting. In fact, crickets were about the only thing he could hunt and catch. Of course, any one can hunt. The hard part of it is to catch what you are hunting.

Tommy was glad that he knew how to capture crickets, for he was very fond of them. To be sure, it took a great many crickets to satisfy his hunger. But they were good when he wanted a light lunch; and there was fun, too, in hunting them.

This is the way Tommy Fox caught crickets. He would stand very still in the tall grass and watch sharply. Wherever he saw the grass moving, Tommy would pounce upon that spot, bringing his two front paws down tight against the ground. And in the bunch of grass that lay beneath his paws Tommy almost always found a fat cricket.

There was just one drawback about that kind of hunting. He could catch crickets only upon still days, when there was no wind; because when the wind blew, the grass waved everywhere, and Tommy couldn't tell whether it was crickets or whether it was wind that made the grass move.

Well, upon this very day when Tommy Fox was amusing himself, and swallowing crickets as fast as he could grab them, his mother came out of her house and watched him for a little while. Tommy was feeling quite proud of his skill.

"I can hunt—can't I, Mother?" he exclaimed. "Watch me! I get them almost every time!" he boasted.

Mrs. Fox did not answer. She was thinking deeply. She knew that there were a great many things she must teach her son, because he was growing up; and some day he would be leaving home to go out into the world and take care of himself. And Mrs. Fox knew that Tommy would have to learn to catch bigger things than crickets in order to keep from starving.

Pretty soon Mrs. Fox started across the field. She was gone rather a long time. But she came back at last, carrying something that squirmed and twisted and wriggled. Whatever it was that Mrs. Fox was bringing home, it was furry, and quite big and heavy. When Tommy saw it he stopped hunting crickets at once. He knew what his mother had. It was a woodchuck!

"Hurrah!" he shouted. "I'm hungry! May I eat all of him I want?" You might think that he had swallowed so many crickets that he wouldn't want anything more to eat just then. But to tell the truth, it was very seldom that Tommy Fox wasn't hungry as a bear.

"Not so fast!" Mrs. Fox said. "I'm going to teach you to hunt. And you're to begin with this woodchuck. Now I'm going to let him go, and you must catch him." So Mrs. Fox let the woodchuck slip away; and off he scampered, with Tommy after him. Mrs. Fox followed close behind. And soon she saw Tommy give a great spring and land right on top of the woodchuck.

Tommy was greatly excited. But he was hungry, too, "May I eat him now?" he asked.

"No! Let him go again," his mother commanded. "And see if you can catch him more quickly next time."

Tommy obeyed. And though he overtook the woodchuck sooner, he was not so careful to avoid the 'chuck's sharp teeth, and he got a savage nip right on his nose.

Tommy was surprised. He was so surprised that he dropped the woodchuck. And you may believe that Mr. Woodchuck lost no time. He scurried away as fast as his legs would carry him.

Tommy began to whimper. His nose hurt; and he thought he had lost his dinner, too.

But Mrs. Fox bounded after Mr. Woodchuck and brought him back again. She made Tommy stop crying. And he had to begin his lesson all over again.

When Mrs. Fox thought that Tommy had learned enough for that day they both sat down and made a meal of that unfortunate Mr. Woodchuck. And Tommy felt that he had already become a mighty hunter. He hadn't the least doubt that he could go into the woods and catch almost anything he saw.

We shall see later whether Tommy Fox knew as much as he thought he did.

IV

MOTHER GROUSE'S CHILDREN

The very next day after his first lesson in hunting, when his mother had brought home the live woodchuck, Tommy Fox went off into the woods alone. He had made up his mind that he would surprise his mother by bringing home some nice tidbit for dinner—a rabbit, perhaps, or maybe a squirrel. He wasn't quite sure what it would be, because you know when hunting you have to take what you find—if you can catch it.

Tommy Fox hadn't been long in the woods before he had even better luck than he had expected. He was creeping through a thicket, making no noise at all, when what should he see but that sly old Mother Grouse, with all her eleven children! They were very young, were old Mother Grouse's children; and they hadn't yet learned to fly. And there they were, all on the ground, with the proud old lady in their midst.

Tommy Fox was so pleased that he almost laughed out loud. He tried to keep still; but he couldn't help snickering a little. And old Mother Grouse heard him. She started to fly. But instead of tearing off out of danger, she lighted on the ground quite near Tommy.

"How stupid of her!" he thought. "I'll just catch the old lady first, and then get the youngsters afterward. They can't fly away."

So Tommy made a leap for old Mother Grouse. He just missed her.

She rose in the nick of time and slipped away from him. But she didn't fly far. So Tommy followed. And he stole up very slyly; and once more, when he was quite near the old lady, he sprang at her.

It was really very annoying. For again old Mother Grouse just escaped. Again she flew a little further away, lighted on the ground, and seemed to forget that Tommy Fox was so near.

That same thing happened as many as a dozen times. And the twelfth time that Mrs. Grouse rose before one of Tommy's rushes she didn't come down again. She lighted in a tree. And since it appeared to Tommy that she had no intention of leaving her safe perch, he gave up in disgust. He was very angry because he hadn't caught old Mother Grouse. But there was her family! He would get them—the whole eleven of them! And he turned back toward the place where he had first come upon them.

Now, sly old Mother Grouse had played a trick on Tommy Fox. If he had just left her alone he could have caught every one of her children. But she had tempted him to follow her. And every time she rose from the ground and flew a short distance, she led Tommy further away from her little ones.

Tommy had some trouble in finding the exact spot where he had stumbled upon Mrs. Grouse and her children. But he found it again, at last. And little good it did him; for not a trace of those eleven young grouse could he discover. They had all disappeared—every single one of them! They knew what to do when their mother led Tommy Fox away. Each of them found a safe hiding-place. Some of them burrowed beneath the fallen leaves; some of them hid behind old stumps; some of them crept into a hollow log. And try as he would, Tommy Fox was unable to find so much as one downy feather.

He was so disappointed—and so ashamed—that he went home and stayed there. But he had learned something. Yes! Tommy Fox knew that if he ever met old Mother Grouse and her family again he would catch her children first. Afterward he would try to capture the sly old lady herself. But he didn't believe, just then, that he would ever be able to catch her. You see, Tommy realized that he wasn't quite so clever as he had thought.

V

TOMMY FOX IS HUNGRY

Tommy Fox kept a sharp look-out to see what he could capture to eat. But he could discover nothing at all. To be sure, there were birds in the trees, and birds' nests too, and Tommy was very fond of birds' eggs. But he couldn't climb trees. The birds were out of his reach; and so were the squirrels. He saw plenty of red squirrels, and gray squirrels, and little striped chipmunks. They looked down from the branches and chattered and scolded at him. They were perfectly safe, and they knew it.

Tommy Fox sat down to think. As I have said, he was hungry. And there is nothing that sharpens a fox's wits like hunger. He looked very innocent, as he rested under a big chestnut tree, and gazed up at a gray squirrel which was perched on a limb over his head.

"Run along, Tommy Fox," the squirrel said to him. — "There's no use of your staying here. I shan't come down until you're gone."

Tommy didn't say anything. He just whined a few times, and held his paw against his stomach. And he gave one or two groans.

The gray squirrel came a little further down the tree and looked at Tommy again. He wondered if Tommy was ill. And then, when Tommy stretched himself out on the ground and lay quite still the gray squirrel was sure that Tommy Fox had eaten something that hurt him.

"What is it?" the squirrel inquired.

Tommy looked up and murmured something. The squirrel couldn't hear what he said, but he thought he caught the word poison. And he decided that Tommy had probably devoured a poisoned chicken-head which Farmer Green had thrown out for him.

I am afraid that the squirrel didn't feel very sorry. He didn't like

Tommy Fox, for Tommy was always trying to catch him. But if he wasn't

sorry, he was curious. And he sat up on a low branch and looked at

13

Tommy for a long time.

Tommy Fox never moved again. His eyes were shut; his beautiful red tail, with its white tip, lay limp on the ground; and his legs stuck out as stiff as pokers.

Mr. Gray Squirrel felt sure that Tommy was very ill. He called and called to Tommy. But he got no reply. And at last he decided that Tommy must be dead. So he slipped down the tree to the ground, to get a better look.

At first Mr. Gray Squirrel stayed close to the tree, so that he could scamper up again in case he was mistaken. But Tommy Fox never moved an eyelash. And at last Mr. Gray Squirrel grew quite bold. He edged closer to Tommy. He had never been so near a fox before, and he was curious to see what he looked like. He stole up beside Tommy and was just about to call to his friends in the next tree-top to come down, when he received the surprise of his life.

As Mr. Gray Squirrel watched, he thought he saw one of Tommy Fox's eyelids quiver. And a great fear seized him. Had he been mistaken? Was Tommy Fox playing dead?

VI

MR. GRAY SQUIRREL'S MISTAKE

Mr. Gray Squirrel certainly was mistaken, when he thought that Tommy Fox was dead and came down out of the chestnut tree to look at him. Tommy wasn't even ill. You remember that he was very hungry? And that he had not been able to find anything to eat? Tommy could not climb the tree, where Mr. Gray Squirrel sat. So the only thing left for him to do was to make Mr. Gray Squirrel come down where he was.

That was what Tommy Fox was thinking about, when he sat there on his haunches and looked up so innocently at Mr. Gray Squirrel. As Tommy sat there a bright idea came to him. So he held his paw to his stomach and pretended to be ill. And as soon as he saw that Mr. Gray Squirrel thought he was ill, Tommy fell over on his side and made believe he was dead.

Though his eyes were shut tight, Tommy's ears were so sharp that he could tell when Mr. Gray Squirrel came down the tree. And he could hear him slowly picking his way nearer and nearer. Tommy's nose was sharp, too, and he could smell Mr. Gray Squirrel. He smelled so good that Tommy couldn't help opening one eye the least bit, just to see him. That was when Mr. Gray Squirrel noticed that his eyelid quivered. And Tommy saw at once that Mr. Gray Squirrel had caught that flicker of his eyelid, and that he was frightened. Tommy knew then that he must act quickly.

He jumped up like a flash. But quick as he was, Mr. Gray Squirrel was even quicker. He reached the tree just ahead of Tommy Fox; and though Tommy leaped high up the trunk, he was too late. Mr. Gray Squirrel scrambled up the tree so fast that his big, bushy tail just whisked across Tommy's face. And in another second he was safe in the tree-top, chattering and scolding, and calling Tommy names.

Tommy Fox felt very foolish. He realized that if he had jumped up without first opening his eye he would not have given Mr. Gray Squirrel any warning; and then he would have caught the plump old fellow. But it was

15

too late now. Another time he would know better. And he sneaked off, to try the same trick on one of Mr. Gray Squirrel's friends.

It was no use. Mr. Squirrel followed him, jumping from one tree-top to another, and made a great noise, calling after him, and jeering at him, and telling all his friends about the mean trick Tommy had tried to play on him.

And to Tommy's great disgust, an old crow high up in a tall tree heard the story, and haw-hawed loudly, he was so amused. He made such a racket that all the forest-people heard him; and Tommy knew that there was no sense in trying to catch a squirrel around there that day. He went down into the meadow and began hunting crickets. And though he didn't have as good a lunch as he wanted, probably he ate all that was good for him.

VII

TOMMY CHASES MR. WOODCHUCK

Tommy Fox went up into Farmer Green's back-pasture, which, lay even nearer Blue Mountain than the field where Tommy and his mother lived. He skulked along among the rocky hummocks, and the old stumps which dotted the pasture thickly. His ears and his eyes and his nose were all alert to discover any small animal that might be stirring—especially his nose; for Tommy could smell things when they were a long way off.

Tommy's mother had explained to him that he must always hunt with the wind blowing in his face; because then the breeze brought to him the scent of any animal that might be in front of him, whether it happened to be an animal that Tommy was hunting, or some animal that was hunting him. In that way Tommy would be able to know what was ahead of him, even if he couldn't see it.

But if he were careless, and trotted along with the wind blowing behind him—ah! that was quite different. The other forest-people would all know he was coming, for then they would be able to get Tommy's scent. And some day, if he were so foolish as to go about with the wind at his back, some day he might stumble right onto a wildcat, or a dog, or a man, or some other terrible creature.

Well—Tommy remembered all these things that his mother had told him. The wind blew fresh in his face. And to his delight all at once he smelled a woodchuck. There was no mistaking that savoury smell. It affected Tommy very pleasantly—much as you are affected by catching a whiff of hot peanuts, or pop-corn, or candy cooking on the stove.

Tommy stole along very carefully. And as he peered around a stump he saw, not ten jumps ahead of him, a fine, fat woodchuck. Tommy crept up a little closer; and then he sprang for Mr. Woodchuck with a rush.

Pudgy Mr. Woodchuck saw Tommy just in time. He turned tail and ran for his life; and he was so spry, though he was quite a fat, elderly gentleman, that he reached his hole and whisked down out of sight just as Tommy was about to seize him.

Tommy was disappointed. But he was determined to get that woodchuck, and he began to dig away at Mr. Woodchuck's hole. You see, Mr. Woodchuck was smaller than Tommy Fox, and since the underground tunnel that led to his home was only big enough to admit him, Tommy was obliged to make it larger. Though Mr. Woodchuck's hole was under a shady oak tree, Tommy found digging to be somewhat warm work, so he took off his neat, red coat and hung it carefully upon a bush.

He worked very hard, for he was eager to find Mr. Woodchuck. In fact, the further Tommy dug into the ground the more excited he grew. And he had just decided that he had almost reached the end of the tunnel, and that a little more digging would bring him inside of Mr. Woodchuck's house, when he met with an unexpected check.

To Tommy's dismay, Mr. Woodchuck's tunnel led between two roots of the big oak, and Tommy could not squeeze between them. He reached his paws through the narrow opening and crowded his nose in as far as it would go. But that was all he could do. He did not doubt that somewhere in beyond, in the darkness, Mr. Woodchuck was having a good laugh because Tommy had done all that work for nothing.

I am sorry to say that Tommy Fox lost his temper. He called after Mr. Woodchuck. Yes—he shouted some rather bad names after him. But of course that didn't do a bit of good. And Tommy Fox put on his coat and went home to think about what he could do. He didn't care to ask his mother's advice, because he didn't want her to know that Mr. Woodchuck had got away from him. But he hoped to find some way in which he could catch the old gentleman.

VIII

SOMETHING MAKES TOMMY VERY PROUD

Tommy Fox could think of nothing but Mr. Woodchuck. He thought there could be no use in going back to the hole beneath the big oak in the pasture until the next day, because Mr. Woodchuck would probably be afraid that Tommy was waiting for him to come out. Yes—Tommy decided that Mr. Woodchuck would stay in his house down among the roots of the big tree and not show himself again until he felt quite sure that his enemy had grown tired of watching and had given up the idea of catching him.

But Tommy guessed that by another day old Mr. Woodchuck would be so hungry that he would have to go out of doors again to get something to eat. And Tommy Fox could hardly wait for the night to pass. But another day came at last; and it found Tommy up and hurrying to Farmer Green's back-pasture, where Mr. Woodchuck lived. It was just growing light; and there was a heavy dew upon the grass, which Tommy didn't like at all, because he just hated to get his feet wet.

Tommy did not go near Mr. Woodchuck's hole. Although he was just a young fox, he was too wise to do that. He knew that if he went nosing around Mr. Woodchuck's dooryard the old gentleman would smell his tracks as soon as he poked his head out. So Tommy was careful to keep away from the hole where he had dug so hard the day before. He sneaked around until he had passed Mr. Woodchuck's house; and then he crept up behind the big oak close by. And there he waited.

Tommy kept smiling. He was so pleased, because his plan was working out very well. The wind blew towards him, and Tommy saw that Mr. Woodchuck wouldn't be able to smell him when the old fellow came up into the open air.

For a long time Tommy waited there. He kept very still. And he stayed hidden behind the tree, with only one eye peeping round the tree-trunk, so that he could watch for Mr. Woodchuck. He was very patient—was

Tommy. You have to be patient, you know, when you are hunting. He crouched behind the tree for at least an hour, and never once took his eye off that hole. And at last he saw Mr. Woodchuck's nose come popping out.

If Tommy hadn't been watching very closely he wouldn't have seen it at all; for Mr. Woodchuck just stuck his head up for a second, took one quick look all around, and jumped back again. He hadn't seen anything to frighten him. But he thought it best to be very careful.

Tommy waited. And pretty soon that small nose came sticking out again. This time it stayed longer. And to Tommy's great delight, in another minute he saw Mr. Woodchuck climb up and take a good look all about.

Tommy Fox hardly breathed. He didn't see how the old gentleman could help spying him. But he didn't. And then Mr. Woodchuck started off across the pasture, to find something for breakfast. He was very hungry, for he hadn't had any supper the night before.

Tommy Fox waited until Mr. Woodchuck had gone just a few steps away from his doorway. And then Tommy stole after him. This time Tommy was between Mr. Woodchuck and his house. And Mr. Woodchuck couldn't escape.

It was all over in a second. And Tommy Fox felt very proud of himself when he reached home and showed his mother what he had brought.

"I can hunt—can't I, Mother?" he said. "To-morrow I'm going up on the mountain and catch a bear."

"Don't be silly," Mrs. Fox said. "You know you couldn't catch a bear."

But she was much pleased, in spite of what she said. For she saw that

Tommy was really beginning to learn something.

IX

TOMMY FOX IN TROUBLE

A few days after Tommy Fox caught old Mr. Woodchuck, something happened that set him thinking. Perhaps I should say "a few nights" instead of "days." For one night his mother came home with a fat hen slung across her shoulders. She had been down to Farmer Green's hen-house, right in the middle of the night, when Farmer Green and his family were asleep; and she had snatched one of the sleeping hens off the roost and stolen away with it without waking anybody.

Only a very wise old fox could do that. "You mustn't go near Farmer

Green's hen-house," Mrs. Fox said to Tommy, as they picked the bones

of the fat hen together. "You are not old enough to get one of Farmer

Green's hens."

You notice that Mrs. Fox didn't speak of "stealing" a hen. She called it "getting" one. For foxes believe that it is only fair to take a farmer's hen now and then, in return for killing field-mice and woodchucks, which eat the farmer's grain. But the farmer never stops to think of that. He only thinks of the hens that he loses.

Tommy Fox never said a word while his mother was talking to him. He was very busy, eating. But that was not the only reason why he kept still. He heard his mother's warning, but he thought she was silly. He really believed that he was quite old enough and quite big enough and quite wise enough to go down to Farmer Green's and get a hen himself. After catching old Mr. Woodchuck Tommy felt that he was able to do about everything his mother could do. And he made up his mind right then and there that he would show her. He would pay a visit to the hen-house that very night.

Tommy Fox could not wait for night to come. In fact, he could wait only until the close of day—he was in such a hurry to capture a hen. The sun had scarcely sunk out of sight in the west and the sky was still red, when he crept slyly up to Farmer Green's hen-house.

Tommy had heard that Farmer Green went to bed very early, after working hard in the fields each day. And since he saw nobody stirring about the place he thought that everyone was asleep.

The hens were asleep. There was no doubt of that. Peeping inside their little house, Tommy could see them roosting in rows. And he lost no time in squeezing through one of the small doors. He felt a bit timid, once he was inside. And for a moment he almost wished that he hadn't come. But he was determined to take a hen home with him; so he reached up and grabbed the very first hen he came to, on the lowest perch of all.

It was a big, old, white hen that Tommy Fox seized. She awoke the moment he touched her, and began to squall. And to Tommy's alarm, all the rest of the hens heard her and began to cackle loudly. The noise was deafening. And Tommy made a dash for the little door, with old Mrs. White Hen in his mouth. She was flapping her wings and kicking as hard as she could. And Tommy was dismayed to find that he could not get her through the narrow door. Every time he tried to push through, one of Mrs. White Hen's legs, or a wing, or her head, struck against the edge of the doorway.

Then a dog barked. And Tommy heard something running around the chicken-house. He just knew that it was a man. And he dropped the old hen in a hurry and slipped through the door.

He was just in time. He heard a man shout, "After him, Spot!" And giving one frightened glance over his shoulder, Tommy saw that Farmer Green's dog was close behind him.

X

MRS. FOX OUTWITS DOG SPOT

Poor Tommy Fox! How he wished that he had obeyed his mother, and kept away from Farmer Green's hen-house! Now Farmer Green's dog Spot was chasing him. Tommy could hear him baying joyfully as he followed. But you may be sure that Tommy was not joyful. He was terribly frightened. He could think of nothing to do except to run, run, run! as fast as he could go. He was headed straight for home, and he only hoped that he would get there before the dog Spot caught him.

Now, Tommy was doing just about the worst thing he could do. He never once jumped sideways, or ran around in a circle. And though he might have waded a little way in the shallow brook in the meadow, where Spot would have lost his trail, Tommy used the bridge to get across the stream; so the dog Spot had no trouble at all in following him. And Spot kept drawing nearer and nearer.

It happened that Mrs. Fox heard the baying of the dog. And she knew what Spot was saying. He was crying—"I've almost got him! I've almost got him!"

A shiver passed over Mrs. Fox; for she thought at once of Tommy. He was not at home, and she wondered if by any chance he was in trouble. She hurried through the field to see who it was that Spot was chasing. And sure enough! pretty soon Mrs. Fox saw Tommy come tearing through the field, panting hard, with his tongue hanging out, and a most frightened look upon his face.

Mrs. Fox hastened to meet him. The dog Spot was then on the other side of a low hill, and running along with his nose to the ground.

"Jump!" Mrs. Fox said to Tommy, as soon as he joined her.

Tommy remembered, then, what his mother had always told him. So he gave a long leap to one side.

23

"Now make a big circle, and jump again. Then go home!" That was all Mrs. Fox had time to say. She stopped just long enough to see Tommy dash off; and then she started right in the opposite direction.

The dog Spot saw her and gave a yelp of delight. He did not know what had been happening. He only thought that now he was going to catch the fox, which was the stupidest fox he had ever chased, running as it did, straight away, with never a leap or a circle, or any other sort of trick to fool him. Little did Spot guess that old Mrs. Fox had not the slightest idea of being caught. She had been followed by Spot himself many times; and she knew exactly how to escape him. She just lingered for a few moments, to make sure that Tommy was safe, and that Spot was chasing her. And then how she did run! In no time at all she left Spot far behind.

Now, Mrs. Fox knew that there was a ploughed field nearby, and that was just what she wanted. She scampered towards it at great speed and went straight across it. And when she had reached the other side of the ploughed ground she sat down for a short breathing spell.

You see, Mrs. Fox was very wise indeed. She knew that in dry weather, such as there was then, a ploughed field takes no scent at all. She knew that when Spot reached that loose dirt Spot could not smell her footsteps. And so she just sat there on her haunches, and caught her breath again.

A grim smile crossed Mrs. Fox's face as she heard Spot barking away in the distance. It was a very different bark from what she had heard when he was chasing Tommy. This time Spot was saying, "Oh, dear! oh, dear! I've lost him!" over and over again.

When Mrs. Fox reached home she found Tommy safe inside their house. He

was crying, because he was afraid he would never see his mother again.

And after his mother found out how Spot had happened to chase him,

Tommy cried some more—but for an entirely different reason.

TOMMY GROWS TOO CARELESS

By the time summer was nearly over, Tommy Fox was much bigger than he had been in the spring. So many things had happened, and he had learned so much, that he began to be quite bold. And he had grown so saucy that his mother often had to scold him. Tommy had fallen into the bad habit of going about calling all the forest-people names; and in that way he had gained for himself the ill-will of all the creatures who lived near the foot of Blue Mountain. It interfered with his hunting, because whenever he started out to get something to eat, as soon as they saw him the forest-people told one another that he was coming. Old Mr. Crow especially was the worst of all. He was forever calling "Stop, thief!" after Tommy Fox; and then he would haw-haw in a manner that was frightfully annoying. In fact, he made matters so unpleasant that after a time Tommy began to roam far down the valley, along Swift River, where he tried to catch fish. The fish, at least, couldn't call him names, and there was some satisfaction in that fact, even if he hadn't much luck as a fisherman.

And just for excitement Tommy began to worry Farmer Green's Spot. He delighted in barking at Spot. And Spot would always stop what he was doing and rush pell-mell after Tommy Fox.

Then Tommy would skip away with a laugh. First he always ran for the river, and jumped from one stone to another, and waded where the water was shallow.

Then he would dash off through the meadows, leaving so crooked a trail behind him that when Spot at last found the place where Tommy had left the river, he never could follow him very far.

But one day Tommy stumbled upon Spot quite by accident. There was no wind at all that day, to bring any scent to Tommy's sharp nose. And he suddenly found that Spot was right in front of him, between him and the river.

Tommy Fox turned and ran. He laughed, too; because he felt quite sure that he could outwit old Spot. And he leaped and twisted and turned about, and made so many circles, that he felt sure Spot couldn't follow him.

Yes—Tommy felt so safe that he stopped running and was trotting slowly along through the field in which he lived. He was almost home, when he heard a noise behind him. He looked around and to his great surprise there was Spot almost upon him.

There was no time to lose. There was only one thing Tommy could do. The door of his mother's house was only a short distance off and Tommy made for it. Luckily, he managed to reach it. Once inside, he could hear the dog Spot barking in the opening. But he knew that Spot was too big to follow him.

Although Tommy was very glad to be safe at home, he was worried. For now Spot know where he and his mother lived; and they would have to move. Tommy was afraid his mother would be very angry with him for being so stupid as to let Spot follow him. But he couldn't help it now.

Meanwhile, old Spot continued to bark, and scratch at the door of

Tommy's home. But at last he stopped. And all was still.

Tommy wondered where his mother was. She was not at home. And he wanted to see her, even if he was afraid that she would punish him. For Tommy did not know exactly what to do. He did not dare go out for fear Spot might be lying in wait for him. So Tommy stayed there. And still his mother did not come home. He wondered where she could be.

XII

OLD MR. CROW IS PLEASED

There was a very good reason why Mrs. Fox did not come home that day when the dog Spot chased Tommy Fox into his house. She had heard old Spot barking in the field and she had hurried toward home as fast as she could, to see what was the matter.

To her great dismay, when she leaped up on the stone-wall not far from her house Mrs. Fox could see Spot scratching at her door. And she guessed at once that he had driven Tommy inside.

The poor old lady hardly knew what to do. But she hid in the grass, hoping that Spot would grow tired of his task and go home. But old dog Spot kept up a great barking. He howled so loudly that they heard him way off at the farm-house; and Mrs. Fox nearly wept when she saw Farmer Green and his boy Johnnie come hurrying across the fields.

Pretty soon Johnnie Green returned to the farm-house; and when he came back Mrs. Fox could see that he carried a steel trap. For a short time Johnnie and his father busied themselves at her doorway. And then they went away, calling old dog Spot after them.

After they had gone, Mrs. Fox stole sadly across the field to the home she had liked so well. She knew that she could live there no longer in peace and quiet. Yes—she would have to move. And now the first thing to be done was to get Tommy safely out of the house.

Mrs. Fox reached her door-yard. And there she paused. There was no trap to be seen, anywhere. But the path leading to her door was sprinkled thick with fresh earth; and wise old Mrs. Fox knew that hidden underneath it, somewhere, lay that cruel trap, with its jaws wide open, waiting to catch her if she stepped between them.

She crept as close to her door as she dared, and called softly to Tommy. I don't need to say that her son was delighted to hear his mother's voice. He

27

poked his nose out of the hole at once. And he would have jumped out and fallen right into the trap if his mother had not warned him.

"Don't come out!" she cried sharply, "There's a trap here, beneath this dirt. Now, do just as I tell you, or you'll be caught!"

Tommy Fox was frightened. For once, at least, he believed, that his mother knew more than he did. And he didn't dare move, except when she ordered. He didn't dare put a foot down except where she told him to.

Tommy had taken several careful steps, and his mother had begun to think that he was almost safely past the trap, when a very unfortunate thing happened. Tommy was just about to set one of his front feet down upon a spot that his mother had pointed out to him, when somebody suddenly called, "Stop, thief!"

Tommy Fox was so startled that he gave a quick jump. Snap! went the trap. And though Tommy sprang up into the air, he was just too late. The trap closed tightly across the tips of his toes. It was only one foot that was caught; but that was enough. He could not get away — no matter how hard he pulled.

It was old Mr. Crow who had called "Stop, thief!" He was laughing now. His "Haw-haw! haw-haw!" could be heard plainly enough, as he flapped away in great glee, to tell all the forest-people that Tommy Fox would trouble them no more.

XIII

JOHNNIE GREEN AND HIS NEW PET

Tommy Fox was in a terrible fix. He was caught fast by the foot in a trap; and if that isn't being in a fix, I should like to know what is.

All night long he whimpered and cried. All night long he tugged and pulled, trying to get free. But the more he tugged the more the trap hurt his foot. And the harder he cried.

Mrs. Fox couldn't help Tommy at all. She stayed with him throughout the night, and tried to comfort him. And she only left when morning came and she smelled men coming across the fields. Then, with one last sorrowful look at Tommy, she crept sadly away.

In a few minutes more Farmer Green and his boy Johnnie reached Mrs. Fox's door. And they were both greatly pleased when they saw that the trap had done its work so well.

"It's a young cub," Farmer Green said, as soon as he spied Tommy Fox.

"May I have him, Father?" Johnnie asked quickly. "I'd like him for a pet."

Tommy Fox was terribly frightened when he heard that. You see, he didn't know what a "pet" was. He thought that probably it was something like a stew, for he had been told that people ate things like that; and he could see himself, in his mind's eye, being cut up and tossed into a pot.

"A pet, eh?" said Farmer Green. "Well, I suppose so. He's hardly worth skinning. You may have him, I guess. But look out that he doesn't bite you."

Johnnie Green was delighted. He helped his father put Tommy into an old sack, and taking the trap too, they started toward the farm-house. When they reached Farmer Green's home Johnnie and his father fitted a stout collar about Tommy's neck. And they fastened one end of a chain to it; and the other end they tied to a long stake, which they drove into the ground in Farmer Green's door-yard. Then Johnnie Green set a big wooden box close

29

beside the stake. He tipped the box over on its side, and threw some straw into it. And that was Tommy Fox's new home.

You might think that it was a much nicer home than he had before. But Tommy did not like it at all. All the people on the farm came and looked at him, inside the box; and Johnnie Green never left him for more than ten minutes all the rest of that day.

Tommy made up his mind that he would make a house of his own. And that very night he dug a hole in Farmer Green's dooryard, where he could crawl out of sight of everyone. Tommy liked that much better. No matter how hard Johnnie Green pulled on the chain, he couldn't drag Tommy out unless he wanted to come.

But after a few days Tommy began to get used to being a pet. He found that it was not such a terrible thing, after all. He did miss the fine runs he used to have; and the hunts; and he missed his mother, too. He could hear her often, at night, calling to him from the fields. And then Tommy would answer, and tug at his chain. But he couldn't get away. And after a while he would go to sleep and dream pleasant dreams, about catching crickets in the long grass.

TOMMY FOX MAKES A STRANGE FRIEND

There was one thing, especially, that surprised Tommy Fox. And I think it surprised the dog Spot even more. Tommy and Spot became friends.

At first, whenever Spot came near, Tommy would run into his hole, as far as his chain would allow him. But after a time he began to peep out at his visitor. And finally he grew so bold that when Spot came to see him he stayed above ground, though to be sure he sat close to the door of his house, so that he could whisk out of sight if Spot should come too near him.

Since Spot often came to look at Johnnie Green's new pet, he began to like Tommy. And instead of growling, he would wag his tail, and try to be friendly. And the first thing they knew, they were playing together, and rolling and tumbling about, pretending to bite each other.

Now, Spot was much bigger than Tommy Fox, and stronger. And sometimes when they played together he would get so rough that Tommy would run down into his underground house and hide. But he never lost his temper, because he knew that Spot did not mean to hurt him. And Tommy was always ready to come out again and play some more.

Johnnie Green was very proud of his new pet. And one day when he was going to drive to the village he took Tommy Fox with him. He tied Tommy's chain to the wagon and Tommy sat up on the seat beside his young master. He had a fine ride. It frightened him at first, to see so many people, for it was market-day, when the farmers for miles around came to the village to sell their butter and eggs and vegetables. There was a great number of dogs, too, running about the village streets. Tommy was glad that he was high up on the seat of the wagon, beside Johnnie Green, for he knew that he was perfectly safe there. He saw so many strange sights that after that first day whenever he saw Johnnie starting off for the village he was never satisfied unless he went too.

On the whole, Tommy Fox did not have a bad time, being Johnnie Green's pet. And although Farmer Green often complained that Johnnie would rather play with his young fox than drive the cows, or feed the chickens, or fetch water from the pump, still Farmer Green himself rather enjoyed watching Tommy Fox.

But at last something happened that made Farmer Green very angry. One morning he discovered that a fine hen had disappeared during the night. And the following night another hen vanished.

Farmer Green was puzzled. Old Spot had been loose all the time, and he had never barked once. That was what made Farmer Green suspicious.

Farmer Green went out into his door-yard, where Tommy Fox was basking in the sunshine. Tommy looked up at Farmer Green very innocently. You would have thought he had never done anything wrong in all his life.

Farmer Green began to examine the ground about Tommy's house. He didn't find anything unusual. But when he knelt down and peered into the hole Tommy Fox had dug for himself, what should he see but several hen-feathers!

That was enough for Farmer Green. He knew then where his fat hens had gone. But he was puzzled. There was Tommy, chained fast to the stake. How could he ever have visited the hen-house?

Farmer Green picked up Tommy's chain. And to his surprise he found that the end of it wasn't fastened to the stake at all! It had worked loose, somehow. And Tommy had been free to wander about as much as he pleased.

XV

JOHNNIE GREEN FEELS SAD

Yes—there was trouble when Farmer Green discovered that Tommy Fox had been stealing his hens. He fastened the end of Tommy's chain to the stake once more. And then he went out to the barn, where his boy Johnnie was watering the horses.

"We'll have to kill that fox," he said to Johnnie. "He's got loose, somehow, and he's stolen two hens. I can't have him on the place any longer. He's made friends with old Spot and the dog will let him do anything he likes."

Poor Johnnie Green! He felt so sad! And he begged his father not to kill Tommy. But Fanner Green was very angry with Tommy.

"No!" he said. "That cub's so tricky there's no knowing when he'll get loose again." But Johnnie begged so hard that his father promised that he might keep Tommy one more day.

Johnnie Green was in despair. He could not bear to have his pet killed. And when he went to bed that night he never fell asleep at all. He was very tired; but he managed to keep awake. And in the middle of the night Johnnie got out of bed and put on his clothes. He didn't dare to light his candle. But the moonbeams streamed in through his little gable-window and Johnnie could see very well without any other light.

As soon as he was dressed Johnnie stole down the stairs, carrying his shoes in his hand, so he wouldn't make any noise. In spite of all his caution, the old stairs would creak now and then. But luckily nobody heard him; and soon Johnnie was out of the house.

He found Tommy Fox wide awake, sitting on his haunches in the moonlight, listening. Far away in the distance a fox was barking and Tommy thought it sounded like his mother's voice.

Tommy was surprised to see Johnnie Green at that hour. And he was astonished when Johnnie untied the chain from the stake and started away

33

with him. They went off across the fields, toward Blue Mountain, right in the direction of that barking.

The meadows smelled sweet; and Tommy Fox began to wish that he could slip his head out of his collar and scamper away.

And that was exactly what happened.

After they had gone some distance, Johnnie Green stopped. He unbuckled Tommy's collar, and gave Tommy a push.

At first Tommy was not quite sure that he wanted to leave his good master. But there was that fox, yelping and calling. Something seemed to draw Tommy toward that sound. He just couldn't help himself. And the first thing he knew he was bounding off over the meadow running as fast as his legs would carry him, and barking as loudly as he could bark.

Johnnie Green went slowly home again. He crept into the house and stole upstairs, and cried himself to sleep. But he was glad of one thing. Tommy Fox would not be killed the next morning.

XVI

TOMMY BECOMES BOASTFUL

When Johnnie Green turned Tommy Fox loose, out in the meadow, in the moonlight, Tommy hurried across the fields as fast as he could go. You remember that he heard a fox barking, near the foot of Blue Mountain, and he thought it sounded like his mother. So Tommy barked, too. And as he ran he could hear that other fox coming towards him. Pretty soon they met, and such a joyful meeting you never saw in all your life. For it was old Mrs. Fox. And she was so delighted to see Tommy that she licked him all over with her tongue, and looked at him carefully, to see if he was hurt anywhere. Mrs. Fox had never expected to see Tommy again. But there he was, bigger than ever, and altogether too fat, for Johnnie had fed him well; and then, there were those two hens that Tommy had stolen.

Tommy Fox was very glad indeed to see his mother once more. He frisked about her, and yelped, and jumped up and down. And when she saw that Tommy had come back safe and sound Mrs. Fox danced a little bit, too.

And then she took Tommy home.

You remember that when Farmer Green caught Tommy in a trap, right at the door of his mother's house, Mrs. Fox had been obliged to move. Her new home was not far away from the old one. It was snug and cozy, and on the whole was a pretty nice sort of house, though the dooryard was not quite so sunny as she would have preferred, for the branches of a big tree shaded it.

Tommy had to answer a great many questions. His mother wanted to know everything that had happened to him. She was astonished when she found that he had been in the village, right in the daytime. He was the only fox she knew of who had ever been there. And when she heard of Tommy's friendship with the dog Spot Mrs. Fox was more surprised than ever. She couldn't understand it. And she shook her head over and over again as

35

Tommy told her what good times he and Spot had had together. Mrs. Fox actually began to think that Tommy was telling stories.

The other forest-people, too, thought that Tommy was fibbing when he bragged about his strange adventures. And old Mr. Crow began to cry "Stop, liar!" after him, instead of "Stop, thief!" as he used to do.

But Tommy Fox didn't mind that very much. He knew that he was telling the truth. And he more than half guessed that old Mr. Crow was jealous of him, because he had so many wonderful things to tell.

Though the forest-people always listened to Tommy's stories, they disliked him more than ever. For he was always going about boasting of what he had seen, and what he had done, and what his friend, the dog Spot, said.

"If you're such good friends with old dog Spot, why don't you go down to the farm-yard and see him?" Mr. Crow said to Tommy one day. This was long after Tommy had come back to live with his mother. In fact, it was quite late in the fall, and the weather was growing cold.

"All right! I will!" Tommy said. He was not going to let old Mr. Crow get the better of him. "I'll go now," Tommy said. And with that he started down the valley toward Farmer Green's buildings.

XVII

PAYING A CALL ON A FRIEND

Mr. Crow had dared Tommy Fox to go down to pay a call on his friend dog Spot, at Farmer Green's place. And Tommy was trotting along across the fields. He was quite near Farmer Green's house when he heard a dog bark not far away.

"There's Spot now!" Tommy said to himself. And he turned at once in the direction of the barking. He was smiling, for he knew Spot would be greatly pleased to see him, and very much surprised, too.

Tommy stole slyly up toward the place where the dog was barking. The sound came from beyond some bushes. And Tommy thought he would jump out from behind the bushes and startle Spot. So he crept up to the bushes and then suddenly gave a yelp and leaped clean over them.

It was Tommy Fox himself who got the surprise. For there was a strange dog! And as soon as he saw Tommy he sprang after him.

Tommy did not wait a second. He left that place a great deal faster than he came. And as he went skimming over the fields, a red streak against the brown stubble, he could hear Mr. Crow laughing heartily. The old fellow had sailed along high over Tommy's head, to see what happened; and he was greatly pleased with himself. You see, he knew that Farmer Green's hired man had brought home a new dog just a few days before, and Mr. Crow hoped that if Tommy went to the farm-yard he would meet the strange dog.

Tommy was very angry. He saw at once that old Mr. Crow had tricked him and he made up his mind that if he ever had a chance he would get even with the old gentleman. But now he had no time to think about that. There was that strange dog, following hot on his trail. Tommy had quite enough to worry him, without bothering his head over Mr. Crow just then.

Now, even if Tommy Fox was conceited, he was really a very bright youngster. And as he bounded along he thought of a pretty clever scheme.

37

Yes, he thought of a fine trick to play on that dog. The idea came to him all at once. And as soon as the thought popped into his head, Tommy turned toward Swift River. He was at the bank in no time, and he skipped nimbly down to the river's edge.

Tommy Fox could see no water at all running in Swift River. And you might think he was disappointed. But he wasn't. He found exactly what he had hoped for. He could see no water running, down there in the bed of the river, because the river was covered with ice. It was just a thin shell of ice; but it was strong enough to bear Tommy's weight. He ran across it quickly. And then what do you suppose he did? He sat right down on the opposite bank!

Tommy Fox wanted to see the fun. He had to wait only a minute. For pretty soon the strange dog came rushing down the opposite bank of the river and leaped far out from the edge of the stream.

There was a crash, and a splitting, crackling noise! And the strange dog was floundering in the cold water. The ice was not thick enough to hold him up, and he had hard work to scramble back to the bank again. But he climbed out of the water at last, and tucked his tail between his legs and made off.

Old Mr. Crow saw what happened. He stopped laughing. And he sailed away silently, thinking that Tommy Fox was a pretty smart young cub, after all.

XVIII

THE WORLD TURNS WHITE

After he outwitted the strange dog, Tommy Fox became more of a braggart than ever. He thought that he knew just about all there was to know. But with the coming of winter Tommy found that he had many things to learn. It was almost like living in a different world, for the ground was white everywhere. And though Tommy Fox loved to play in the snow, he discovered one thing about it that he did not like at all. It frightened him when he saw how plainly his footprints showed after a fresh snow-fall. And he wondered how he would ever be able to escape being caught, should any strange dog chase him.

As the winter days passed, Tommy learned that it was very hard for him to run fast in a light, dry snow—that through such snow a dog could run much faster than he could. But when there was a thin crust he could go skipping along like the wind, while dogs, being heavier, broke through the crust and floundered about in the softer snow beneath.

One day Tommy and his mother were out hunting. The snow was very deep everywhere, for it was mid-winter. And it had thawed and frozen so often that the snow was quite hard, except for just about an inch of fresh snow which had fallen during the night. Tommy and his mother could see rabbit tracks all around them; and they had very good luck hunting. But something happened that wasn't exactly lucky. They had turned toward home, when a dog bayed somewhere behind them, and pretty soon Mrs. Fox saw that they were being followed.

She and Tommy started to run. And Tommy saw that there was one more bad thing about winter. Swift River, and all the little brooks, were covered with thick ice and there was no chance at all for him and his mother to run through shallow water and throw the dog off their scent.

It was that strange dog that was chasing them—the one that belonged to Farmer Green's hired man. He was a very fast runner, and in spite of the usual tricks that foxes know, Mrs. Fox and Tommy could not lose him.

Tommy began to be frightened. And old Mrs. Fox herself was somewhat worried. But she still had a few tricks up her sleeve. She didn't intend to let that dog catch them if she could help it.

"Oh, Mother! whatever shall we do?" Tommy said. "Do you think we can get away from him?"

"Of course," Mrs. Fox answered. "But you must do just as I tell you. Now, follow right in my tracks, and don't be frightened, I'm going to show you a new trick—one that my own mother taught me when I was no older than you are."

Mrs. Fox turned to the right and started back across the valley. She was going straight toward Swift River.

"Oh, dear!" Tommy cried. "Don't you know that the river is frozen solid, Mother? The dog can follow us across it, as easy as anything."

"Stop fussing!" Mrs. Fox said, looking over her shoulder at Tommy.

"We're not going to the river. You just mind me and you'll see, in a

few minutes, that we can fool that dog." And she kept on running, with

Tommy right at her heels.

TOMMY FOX LEARNS A NEW TRICK

Now, there was a road that ran through the valley, along the bank of Swift River. And when Mrs. Fox reached it, with Tommy close behind her, she turned again—this time to the left—and ran along in the beaten track which the horses and sleighs had made.

Tommy Fox thought it very strange that his mother should lead him to the road, where they were sure to find people driving. Tommy followed her. But he was very unhappy. They swung into the road just ahead of a farmer, who was driving along in a sleigh. The sleigh-bells tinkled merrily as the horse trotted smartly down the road. But the jingling of the bells did not sound at all pleasant to Tommy Fox. It only frightened him all the more.

The farmer in the sleigh did not see Tommy and his mother, for the snow rose high on both sides, and the road wound in and out. Little did he know that Mrs. Fox and Tommy were scampering along in front of him. Of course, he couldn't catch them, anyhow. Tommy knew that much. But if they ran very far down the road they would be sure to meet some other man.

To Tommy it seemed bad enough to have that dog chasing them, without going where they were sure to find other enemies. Tommy could hear the dog baying. And he knew dogs well enough to know that that dog felt very sure he was going to catch them. But pretty soon Tommy heard the dog talking in a very different fashion. He gave a number of short barks, which meant that he was in trouble.

Mrs. Fox looked over her shoulder and smiled at Tommy. She knew that they were safe. She knew that the dog had not reached the road until the farmer had driven right over their footsteps and spoiled their scent. After the horse had passed over their trail the dog could smell only the horse's footprints, instead of theirs. And Mrs. Fox could tell what was happening back there in the road. She knew just exactly as well as if she had been there herself—she knew that the dog had stopped short, and was running all around, with his nose to the ground, trying to find where she and Tommy had gone. But he never found out.

You see, he wasn't half as clever as Mrs. Fox. It never once occurred to him that Tommy and his mother had turned into the road just ahead of that farmer in his sleigh. And finally the stupid dog gave up the chase and went back to Farmer Green's house.

By that time Mrs. Fox and Tommy were safe at home. Yes—they were even having a good laugh over the way they had fooled the dog. And Tommy had quite forgotten how frightened he had been. In fact, he began to feel very well pleased with himself. For he never once remembered that it was his mother, and not himself, who had thought of that trick. He ought to have felt very grateful to his grandmother, for having taught his mother that clever way of cheating a dog out of his dinner. But Tommy Fox was so conceited that if his grandmother had been there with them he would have thought he knew ten times as much as she did. I've no doubt that he would even have tried to teach her to suck eggs—never once stopping to think that she knew all about such things many years before he was born.

XX

THE DRUMMER OF THE WOODS

Tommy Fox stopped short and listened. It was early spring, and the snow was still deep on the sides of Blue Mountain.

Thump—thump—thump, thump, thump, thump! Rub—rub—rub—rub, r-r-r-r-r-r-r! If you had heard that sound you would have said that there was a boy hidden somewhere on the mountain; and that he was playing a drum. But Tommy Fox knew better than that. He knew that it was Mr. Grouse, calling to Mrs. Grouse. And Tommy knew that he made that noise by beating the air with his strong wings.

Now, Tommy Fox had not eaten a grouse for a long, long time. He had never captured a grouse himself. In fact, he had never even tried, since that time in the summer, when old Mother Grouse had played a trick on him, and led him away from her children.

Tommy made up his mind now that he was old enough and wise enough to capture Mr. Grouse. But he thought he had better wait until night, when Mr. Grouse couldn't see well. Tommy Fox's eyes, you know, were even sharper at night than they were in the daytime.

Well! Tommy Fox went home. And that very night he stole back again to the clump of evergreens where he had heard Mr. Grouse drumming.

It was pretty dark up there on the mountain. But Tommy had no trouble at all in finding his way. And he kept looking up at the thick branches of the evergreens, for he hoped that Mr. Grouse was asleep on a low branch, which he could reach with a good, high jump.

Yes—it was dark. And it was very cold up there on Blue Mountain, for all it was early springtime. And the evergreen trees bowed beneath a burden of snow, which had fallen only the day before.

It was very still in the forest. And when Tommy Fox suddenly heard a cry of "Whoo—whoo—whoo!" he jumped, in spite of himself. Tommy knew,

43

right away, that it was only Mr. Owl. And he felt very sheepish. And then all at once Tommy jumped again. This time he was terribly frightened, for the strangest thing happened. The snow rose right up beneath his feet, and flew in his face. And something struck him a good, hard blow under his chin. Tommy fell over backward in the snow, he was so surprised. And a roar like thunder rang through the forest.

Tommy knew then what had happened. Maybe you have guessed, too. For it was Mr. Grouse himself. He had burrowed his way into the snow, so that he might have a warm blanket to cover him during the night. And Tommy Fox had stepped squarely on top of him.

It was no wonder Mr. Grouse had sprung up in a hurry. He was just as frightened as Tommy himself, because he had been sound asleep, and he had no idea what was the matter.

As for Tommy Fox, it was a huge joke on him. But it was a joke that didn't please Tommy at all. He felt very silly, when it was all over.

XXI

THE BIGGEST SURPRISE OF ALL

It was a pretty big surprise for Tommy Fox, when Mr. Grouse sprang out of the snow, right beneath his feet. But it was nothing at all, compared with the surprise Tommy had when he reached home.

Very late at night Tommy stole into his mother's house. In fact, it was nearly morning. And Tommy crept in very quietly, for he hardly expected that his mother would be awake and he did not want to disturb her.

Tommy had just curled up on his bed and was all ready to go to sleep, when to his great astonishment he heard his mother talking. She was not talking to him, but to someone near her, for she spoke so low that Tommy could not hear what she was saying.

He thought right away that somebody had come to pay them a visit. And he called out—

"Who's here, Mother? Is it a visitor?"

"Yes, Tommy," Mrs. Fox answered. "Come here and see who it is."

Tommy jumped out of bed and hopped across the room. At first he couldn't see anybody but his mother.

"It's just a joke!" Tommy exclaimed. "You're only fooling!"

"Look sharp!" said Mrs. Fox. "It's a surprise. What do you call this?" She moved aside a bit, and pointed to a little, soft, woolly thing which lay close beside her. Tommy had to look two or three times to see what it was. And even then he wasn't sure.

"Is it—is it—a baby?" he asked.

"That's just what it is," his mother said.

Tommy certainly was surprised. And before he could find his voice again Mrs. Fox showed him another baby fox, and another and another and another.

Yes—there they were—five of them all together, small and soft and woolly. They weren't nearly so brightly colored as Tommy and his mother—just a pale, brownish red. Tommy Fox could hardly believe it. As he stared at them he suddenly noticed something strange about the baby foxes. "Why—they're all blind—every one of them!" he cried. "Hadn't we better send them back and get some good ones?" he asked.

Mrs. Fox laughed.

"Of course they're blind," she said. "You were blind when you were their age. Their eyes will be open in a few days…. Well—what do you think of them, Tommy?" she asked; for Tommy Fox seemed to be lost in thought.

"I was wondering how they would ever be able to hunt—they're so small."

"Oh! I'll have to hunt for them, for a long time," his mother explained. "When they get big enough I shall teach them to hunt for themselves, just as I taught you.

"Now you see why I showed you how to catch mice and rabbits and woodchucks," Mrs. Fox said. "You'll have to look out for yourself now, Tommy. For I shall have all I can do to find enough for myself and five children to eat, without feeding a big fellow like you."

That made Tommy Fox feel very proud. He felt bigger, and stronger, and wiser than ever before.

"I shall get along all right," Tommy said. "I almost caught Mr. Grouse tonight. But he got away." Tommy yawned, for he was very sleepy. And pretty soon he was curled up on his little bed again, dreaming of a wonderful bird that he had caught, which was so big that he and his mother and his five little brothers and sisters made a fine meal off it.

But of course it was only a dream.

THE END